Book 2

The God Particle Series

A SIMPLE TALE OF SUBATOMIC PARTICLE
METAPHYSICS

BY PETER LIHOU

Title Verso

The right of Peter Lihou to be identified as the Author
of this work has been asserted by him in accordance
with the Copyright, Designs and Patents Act 1988.

Copyright © Peter Lihou 2012

ISBN-13: 978-1477458310

Cover art by Sam

Published by Acclaimed Books.

www.acclaimedbooks.com

Dedication

To those who choose compassion and challenge dogma.

Preface

Book 2 continues the tale of the elusive God Particles and their human accomplices, 'Honey' and 'Jack'.

The story began at the CERN particle accelerator in 2008 when an attempt was made to launch an experimental program using the brand new and highly sophisticated Large Hadron Collider. During an equipment failure, the first God Particle was created, unbeknown to the scientists. This first particle found its way out of the accelerator and into the computer network at CERN, from where it passed to the World Wide Web.

God Particles have many unusual properties, including the ability to evolve. You might expect that! They also have at their disposal all the information available on the Internet. So before long, it found its way out of the World Wide Web by transforming into an almost human form. It also replicated, enabling many others to join it and at this point chose a name; Book.

Book, not quite a male gender but even less a female, and his friends soon came into contact with humans, in particular with a 'lady of the night' in the West End of London, called 'Honey' and her young son 'Jack'. Unfortunately, they also drew the attention of law enforcement officers when, in Little Rock, Arkansas, their unusual appearance and behaviour aroused concerns of a terrorist threat.

Meanwhile, Book was convinced that there was a purpose in his unique incarnation and after filtering out the advertising and trivia that bombarded him on the Internet, he quickly absorbed the many important scientific discoveries, and profound philosophical insights therein, to arrive at the conclusion that contact must be made with the creator of the universe. This could only be achieved by one of his kind travelling to another dimension. As his friend 'Radio' exhibited many the emotional characteristics of humans and desperately wanted to attempt a transformation that would permit a more meaningful relationship with Honey, Book decided he should be the one.

I very much hope you enjoy reading this tale as much as I am enjoying writing it.

Peter Lihou

Mount View Farm, Bodmin, Cornwall

Radio sat nervously in the centre of a large metal cage that was suspended six feet above the ground by stout ropes secured to the barn rafters. He was attached by a single USB cable, plugged into his side, to a laptop computer on the floor of the cage. The only thing that protruded from the cage was another cable that linked his laptop to another, placed upon a table below.

Chips, Honey and Jack sat patiently in the hay loft from where they commanded an excellent view of their friend. They mouthed subdued reassurances to Radio as Book, below them on the barn floor, tapped away at the connected computer.

"Hold on just a moment longer Radio, we're nearly done." More tapping followed for a few minutes.

"That's it, we're ready to go!"

Just a few days earlier, the scientific community had announced the eagerly awaited conclusion to their search for the mysterious Higgs boson, they had finally found a God Particle. As the world took in the impact of the all important experiment that pin pointed the precise mass of the particle, the greatest scientific thinkers were already formulating further experiments to simulate the immediate aftermath of the Big Bang.

Satisfied with their proof of the so called 'standard model', the scientific community now shifted it's attention to the properties of 'dark matter'.

Unbeknown to them, the released particle made its way out of the Accelerator ring and into the controlling computer network. Very shortly afterwards Book received an email confirming another GP had materialised.

Fortunately, nobody in the scientific community, or anywhere else for that matter, had the slightest inkling that GPs were more than a number, a number that represented their energy in electron volts. Even the Intelligence Agencies, hotly pursuing Woodstock and the others, believed their prey were fanatical terrorists for some, as yet undetermined, cause. With no success to report, Desmond Grapple and his research assistant, Jeffrey, had been recalled to Washington after a particularly dismal Christmas spent in a Bodmin Hotel. Although now assigned to more mundane tasks, they maintained a 'desk watch' for news about the allusive religious sect that appeared to have gone to ground.

"Here we go Radio, see you soon!" Book thought about adding 'hopefully' as he typed into the computer keyboard to start the process. He thought better of it when he saw the distraught expressions on Honey and Jack's faces.

Almost immediately a green mist began to envelope the cage and thirty seconds later, when it dispersed, Radio was gone.

A tear formed in the corner of Jack's eyes as he searched his mother's face for reassurance. But Honey was equally distraught and could only offer a meek smile.

Chips tried to reassure them that Radio would return very soon and all would be well. "It's not like we've killed him. Well OK I suppose it is, but only temporarily."

He was digging himself deeper into a hole when Book yelled excitedly.

"He's made it! He's on the other side, wow! Look at this."

Honey, Jack and Chips jumped down from the loft and rushed across to Book's computer. An email message sprawled across the screen.

'Well that was a blast! Anyway, I'm back here and about to push my way through to the processor. Don't know how long this journey will take but I'll get back to you when I'm ready to return. Radio'

When the initial excitement and relief subsided, a more somber mood set in. Book explained that it might be sometime before they saw their friend again or even received another message from him. As miraculous as the journey back into the computer had been, it was nothing compared to the one upon which he was embarking.

Radio sped from the processor with increased velocity to the port on Book's computer where he traversed onto a cable leading to edge of Book's network. As he approached the modem, travelling at the speed of light, he reflected on the moments before his deconstruction from person (sort of) to particle. He had contemplated the closest experience to death he was likely to know, or so he thought. In those moments of anticipation, Radio's existence became clear and uncluttered. He focused without effort upon his quest and the transformations that lay ahead. He didn't relish the prospect of leaving his friends but his confused emotional state, especially his preoccupation with Honey, needed to be resolved. Returning as a complete human, albeit a God, seemed the answer.

As the world around him; the cage, barn, people he cared for, all began to crumble he followed Book's clear instructions and concentrated on finding the browser session purposely left open. Once back inside the computer, he must attach himself to this session and wait. He would have one minute in which to acknowledge a safe crossing before Book posted a message to the Blog at CERN, a message containing an unexpected passenger.

So far, so good. The draft email containing the acknowledgement required a brief excursion to the keyboard then Radio found his way to the open browser session and waited.

Just under a second later, Radio had been jettisoned through the internet and found himself bombarded on all sides by the network traffic on the host computer of an Internet Service Provider. Several junction boxes, telephone exchange switches, network routers and firewalls had been penetrated en route. It was like sitting in the middle of a motorway junction in the rush hour, only speeded up by several orders of magnitude.

Amid the mayhem, Radio clung to the HTML code that would ensure he made it to his destination at CERN.

Just two more hops across the borders of the Internet and Radio arrived safely at the gateway to a computer server located in an underground data centre near Geneva. The boundary equipment was designed to detect and re-route suspicious code in order to protect the CERN network from hackers, viruses, News International, DDoS and all manner of similar attacks. It had required a good deal of ingenuity on Book's part to design a path through this equivalent to a barbed wire fence and mine field.

Fortunately, Book had access to the entire published knowledge on computer network security at his disposal, on the World Wide Web. Ironic that this was now being used to penetrate the very same data centre where the Web had been invented.

Of course, Book had one enormous advantage over most hackers; his Trojan horse was a subatomic particle!

It therefore required only a minor delay for him to navigate through the firmware and cross into the internal network. Radio was inside the CERN system less than thirty seconds after being posted from the barn. A few seconds later and he had traced a route via the network directory, to the control system for the Large Hadron Collider, where his friend Book had engineered the first escape a few years earlier.

The Farmyard at Mount Farm

Honey had finally settled Jack in bed and persuaded him to at least attempt to sleep. Donning her former 'working girl' attire, she now paced up and down the yard outside the barn where Book maintained a vigilant watch on the computer screen.

As she wobbled on her six inch stiletto heels and worried about Radio and Jack, something else was niggling her. Could her feelings for Radio be more than she had previously admitted to herself? After toning down her dress sense since leaving the street, she wondered what had prompted tonight's wardrobe decision. She didn't need to ponder this point for long. Honey knew 'the uniform', as she often referred to it, was a form of protection - like a suit of emotional armour - against the realities of her street life. When dressed this way, she adopted another persona, one that repressed uncomfortable feelings. That was precisely what she was doing now and the realisation made her feel foolish and just a little vulnerable.

She could wait no longer and barged into the barn, causing Book to almost fall off his stool in surprise.

"Well Honey, I know you like to make an entrance but could you ease up a little? And what's with the outfit, are you going to a fancy dress party or resuming your former career?"

She stood completely still for a moment then meekly apologised, causing Book even more concern for her state of mind.

"I'm sorry, that was selfish of me. I forgot you would be concentrating on that thing." She pointed towards the computer screen.

"I'm not going anywhere and as for the outfit; just a temporary lapse of concentration. You see I'm worried about Jack. He keeps asking questions about Radio; where will he actually be, will he definitely return and how long will it be? I'm… I mean he's also very curious about what Radio is going through. Can he see and hear, what's it like being a particle?"

Her Freudian slip wasn't missed by Book but he chose to ignore it and turned on his stool to face her.

"Sit down Honey, we may be in for quite a wait. Let me explain a couple of things for you.

"I can't be entirely certain but I expect by now he will be inside the computer network at CERN, maybe even inside the Large Hadron Collider itself. I suspect he's still in this Universe though."

Honey's jaw dropped but before she could speak, he continued.

"He needs to cross into another dimension to discover if what you know as God is there, or if the phenomena is exclusive to this one. When he does that, cross over I mean, he'll temporarily take over the LHC and the scientists running it will freak out. That's how we'll know he's gone, it will be all over the news."

"But where exactly is this 'other dimension'?"

Book tried to imagine whether the person dressed in what barely passed as a skirt with a leopard skin blouse immodestly open, would be capable of understanding what he was about to reveal. This concern must have come across because Honey was starting to look embarrassed. Somewhat patronisingly, he began.

"You see Honey, what humans don't yet understand is the relationship between consciousness and matter. 'Dark matter' to be precise. So when a particle collision occurs, naturally or in the LHC, it isn't only particles that are created. Their antithesis, which has so far remained undetected, also results from a collision. The scientists think this is a so called Higgs Field, the force that gives all particles mass. But it's just dark matter and it's part of every Higgs boson - us. The scientists are getting close to understanding this and one has even conceptualised a particle with its own antimatter, the Majorana fermion, but they're not quite there yet.

"It's also part of you. It's your consciousness. Think for a moment about when you first awaken from a deep sleep. Sometimes, when your body is totally relaxed, your only perception is the thought playing out in your mind. When we were inside, as Radio is now, it was like that. We don't have senses; vision, hearing, taste or smell. We don't feel pain or hunger, heat or cold, and we don't experience fear or become excited, we just are. But like your awakening, there's consciousness. That's what it's like for him now.

"Radio must follow a path to a deeper level of consciousness in order to emerge in another dimension. It's like he's on an island but connected to the seabed and if he can just walk across it to another island, he'll emerge in another dimension. The other islands, or dimensions, are normally cut off by the sea between them and in this metaphor the sea is the limitation of human consciousness."

Honey raised her hand a few inches to gesture that he should pause for a moment. He could see she was thinking something through before she spoke.

"So this sea bed is like Jung's Collective Unconscious?"

This time it was Book's jaw that dropped. When he recovered from the shock, he remembered Honey saying she'd been a psychology graduate before her more colourful career. 'Difficult to find the balance between baffling people and being condescending', he thought.

"Exactly. Jung was way ahead of his time. Anyway, if you think the GPs have access to a vast amount of knowledge in the Internet, imagine what Radio might discover when he arrives in the collective unconscious, from where all memory is drawn and has been since the beginning of time."

"When you say, 'all memory', what exactly do you mean?"

"Oh yes, another thing humans haven't quite worked out yet. You'll remember from your psychology studies the good old 'nature verses nurture' arguments, and the debates over the importance of socialisation? Well they kind of pivot on the central question of what behaviour, or anything else for that matter, is learned and what is innate. Humans think that most behaviour is learned but struggle to understand questions like; how do new born babies know to breath, to react to their mother's breast, how do they know how to feed for that matter? The instinct to cry is also thought to be innate as it's the way a baby communicates. But if a newly born infant is really a blank canvas, how would the child know there was somebody to cry to?"

"The idea that behaviour can be passed genetically doesn't exactly fit with how biological systems are understood. So imagine Jung's Collective Unconscious contains all this information and your conscious memories simply draw upon it when your filters allow it. You see, everyone is connected and has access to the same pool of information, or 'seabed' if you stretch the earlier analogy. Babies draw upon it for their basic needs before they begin to reason, humans access as much of this vast store as their filters will allow.

"Imagine a computerised storage system and the vast capacity that would be required to store all the data from just one day of human experience. When you think of the amount of data humans have access to throughout their lives, there is no way their brains could store this let alone index it to allow almost instantaneous recall. The brain would just be too small, physically.

"As for socialisation, babies are born into very different environments. Some have loving parents and plentiful nutrition, others lack both of these. Some have the benefit of great role models; others attach themselves to poor examples of the human race. These varied circumstances have a huge impact on the filters children put in place. Initially open minds become partially or almost totally closed, good or bad influences create 'noise' in their communication channels, both verbal and non-verbal, that shape the growing individual. You can see the eventual outcome when you look at the adults. We often give adults a hard time. People who've benefitted from the good vibes, like to think it's all down to their own efforts and offer no end of theories about life's failures, all of which are designed to validate their own self-worth. Being successful, however you define it, is mostly down to luck. The brow beaten, worn out, failures still have the infants inside them, they've just lost touch with them and years of socialisation has taken its toll."

Book was on a role and about to embark on an explanation of how removing the filters might benefit everyone, when he realised it was now very late and Honey could barely keep her eyes open.

"You need some sleep Honey. Don't worry, I'll keep an eye on the computer."

"Thanks Book, I'm sorry but I am exhausted all of a sudden and I don't want to drop off in this outfit. Jack wouldn't like it if he saw it in the morning."

Jack was fast asleep when she checked his room and as soon as her head hit her pillow, she was too.

The next morning she awoke quite late and lay in her bed thinking about what Book had said. She tried to imagine just being, but a rumbling in her anatomy kind of spoiled the moment. She needed breakfast. Slipping on a dressing gown, she wandered through the farmhouse.

Jack's bed was empty and when she saw he wasn't around in the house, she forgot breakfast and made straight for the barn. The door was open and everyone, including Jack was huddled around the computer screen.

They were clearly excited. Book's voice rang out.

"There you are see, the BBC, ITV, CNN, it's all over the place."

Honey asked what all the excitement was about and when Jack turned to see her, he ran to her and yelled, "he's done it, he's through!"

Chips and the others moved aside so that Book could see her and explain.

"Just like I said, it's all over the news. Something has happened at CERN and the world's media are busy speculating on what that something might be."

Jack burst in again, "he's taken complete control of the Large Hadron Collider and all the computer systems, and they're in a complete panic!"

CIA Major Incident Headquarters Berkeley Virginia, USA

Since their ignominious return to duties in the USA, agent Desmond Grapple and his research assistant, Jeffrey had been split up and whilst Desmond was technically still assigned the task of hunting down those mysterious hoody types, Jeffrey had been moved into a more clerical role.

It was however in this role that Jeffrey was told to liaise with GCHQ in Cheltenham, England when news first broke about the takeover of the LHC. The scientific team at CERN was multinational and despite being some of the brightest people on the planet, security wasn't their forte. When their computer screens failed to respond to any keyboard input and a myriad of unfamiliar symbols appeared, a decision was quickly made by the management team to contact the sponsoring Governments. The CIA embarked upon a risk assessment and created a task force to determine whether the collider could be used to create some kind of nuclear explosion. Meanwhile, GCHQ was tasked with sifting through communications intelligence to try and establish who was behind the hijack. Needless to say, the Taliban was in poll position on the suspect list but other fundamentalist religious groups also ranked highly. Due to the co-operation that existed, it was considered unlikely a foreign power could be involved but Iran and North Korea remained on the list.

Jeffrey had been called in at one o'clock in the morning to assist with the classification of intelligence, specifically from GCHQ. The open plan office was in mayhem as researchers rushed from desk to desk and phones rang constantly. Desperately trying to keep awake, he read the latest email.

Subject: Network traffic T-8 hours

Jeffrey

In the hours prior to this event, communications were heavy due to the experimental activity involving the LHC. The enclosed report documents the IP addresses of every inbound and outbound communication, and where known, the name of the party. We will have any unknown names with you by 1100 hours. There is no evidence of Trojan Horse activity or hacking and the loss of control is not linked to a Botnet or other DDoS attack.

Douglas

Enc. NWT-8. V1.00.pdf

Jeffrey opened the list and began wading through the incoming communications for anything suspicious.

Meanwhile, the situation at CERN was developing further. The director issued a statement to the world's media.

"Further to earlier reports indicating an attack on our computer systems, I have to report a more serious development. At six am European Standard Time, the Large Hadron Collider began to operate in a manner

that is completely unauthorised and contrary to its original design. It appears to be operating, of it's own volition, in reverse.

"As you will appreciate, this latest development is extremely worrying and the continued denial of access to our systems is causing considerable delay to our experimental programs. Following so closely behind the discovery of Higgs boson and the validation of the Standard Model, we had much planned. In particular, further investigations into the properties of dark matter. These have been seriously disrupted and due to the loss of control of our computers, months of stored data that has not yet been fully analysed may have to be scrapped. We'll know more when control is regained."

By issuing the statement without inviting the world's media to a meeting, the director dodged the inevitable questions and speculation about who might be responsible or how long the systems would be unavailable.

Universe 4

From the void a rhythm emerged, the rhythm that created a sense of time. Periodically consciousness kindled and extinguished, at first just a glimmer of faded light, then the light became gradually stronger. No thoughts, but feelings were already forming, feelings prompted by the muffled sounds. Sleeping a while then waking drowsily to hear the sounds. The beat continued in the warm and comfortable space, then movement and an awareness of limbs. Occasionally shuffling around, and then sleeping, all the time a continuous flow of nourishment and a growing awareness of form.

Repeating sounds became familiar, providing a sense of security. There was a gentle, musical, reassuring attention and a sense that the attention was targeted precisely at this form.

The space started to become restrictive and there was a much greater sense of form. Limbs could be moved at will and there was even some control over how the form lay. More space was needed now and there were strong feelings to prepare, for what, the form had no idea. But the form was now aware of its existence and could experience, without understanding, the space and the diffused light glowing around it.

Moving fingers, lots of sensations now and with the sensations there was a growing sense of time. The beat was more present, sounds became more vivid, the diffused light, less diffused, the body feelings more pronounced. The space began contracting; there was a slight movement. More contraction, more movement, the sounds became increasingly urgent.

Pressure, pressure, movement, noise, pressure, sliding, something was happening, pressure, movement – light, bright light, undiminished noise, a slap, gasps, the form was heaving inside as well as out. Its cry was urgent, 'help me, protect me'. The familiar attention was there again and now hugely vivid, it could feel softness, comfort and nourishment. Then there was sleep and exhausted oblivion.

In the first hours and days, the baby breathed instinctively, fed and sensed the environment around it.

As memory functions developed, the growing brain captured every detail of the surroundings vividly and with a clarity that might only diminish years into the future. Learning from the surroundings, the nourishment, protection and the communication of parents was unprompted and unguarded. But there was something about this baby boy that was different. His eyes were too knowing for a newborn.

Jem and her partner, Rock, carried the infant from the birthing room into the main accommodation wing. In the months and years ahead, the child would spend much of his time here before attending the learning sessions in another wing.

The extended family and friends were delighted when the baby's name was announced; 'Zaru' had been the name of an ancestor renowned for his wisdom. Jem told them the choice had been natural because his eyes already seemed so wise.

Zaru flourished and joined the learning sessions well ahead of the usual age, he was seven years old. The people believed that formal education should only begin after a long period of play learning. Zaru had exhausted the benefits of tree climbing, swimming in the river and generally running wild with his friends. He had started to crave information, especially about science and philosophy.

"Tell me again about the other Dimensions mother."

Jem welcomed his curiosity and was keen to explain what they knew about the parallel universes, which were often referred to as Dimensions.

"Well let's see, there are five that we know about so far but our searchers feel confident there are many more we just haven't found yet."

"And do people in those universes know about us?"

"The fifth dimension knows about all of us but the rest don't know. However, one dimension is getting very close to discovering our existence, it may only be a matter of fifty years or so before they break through."

Jem would sit with him for hours explaining their world by drawing pictures on parchment held in frames, using coloured pencils.

The community of people lived in great wooden buildings amid gently rolling hills. There was a clean river nearby and the climate was pleasant all the year around. They were one of many such communities spread around their world, a world without territorial, political, economic, religious or any other boundaries.

Over the ensuing years, Zaru discovered how their communities had evolved from the times when their earliest ancestors had lived in the abundant forests that then covered their planet. As tree dwellers, they rarely stood completely upright and used all four limbs to travel between the trees. In those days the climate was far from pleasant, there was intense competition for food and the threat from predictors was constantly present. Their ancestors moved onto the plains and over time they developed a more upright posture to adapt to their new surroundings. Without the cover of the forest, they felt exposed and so grouped together for security.

On the many cold and dangerous nights spent on the plains, their communication skills grew rapidly and, realising the benefits of working together, they began to organise themselves for the common good. They built shelters, farmed the land and protected their fledgling communities from danger. Although settlements were diversely spread, the people were aware of the futility of confrontation, there were enough challenges in the natural world. These challenges became the focus of those in the communities who were more inclined towards contemplation than physical exertion, many of these were the elders. But one, around three thousand years earlier had just reached his twenties when he began to enlighten the community. He was Zaru's namesake.

In those early times, when death was a common neighbour and the power of the elements dictated so much in their lives, some began to postulate the idea that everything might be determined by supernatural beings; Gods. How else, they argued, could the stars in the night sky so predictably repeat their patterns; especially the great star that dominated their days and seemed inextricably linked to their seasons.

Soon these theories became more elaborate and fused with a concept that would bring comfort to those who feared death the most. If the supernatural beings existed, there was life in another place beyond their world and this was surely where they would be delivered when they died.

The people took solace in this and released from the fear, the existential doubts that had never previously been far from the surface. They soon began to bestow meaning on the movements of celestial bodies and interpret unusual events as messages from the Gods. Diverse communities witnessed widely differing climatic events and so these events and their interpretations also differed. The more articulate members in the communities were called upon to explain to ordinary people what they should believe.

Back then, Zaru was born and raised by a family who lived on the fringe of two communities with competing doctrines. Bickering between the communities had simmered for sometime until one year, their disagreement reached a head.

To the West, they read the heavenly signs as instructions to extensively plough the land, but the community in the East wanted the fields to lay fallow. Zaru was twenty-one years of age when he and his friends listened to the arguments from the circle of elders from both communities. The nub of it seemed to be that one group was convinced the Gods were using a shooting star as a sign to plough, and others regarded an uncharacteristic period of snow the previous winter as a warning to leave the fields to rest for the season. Neither side showed any indication that they'd be willing to compromise.

To Zaru, the argument seemed ridiculous but he kept his own council and slipped away from the gathering. He walked across the plains to a hill from which both settlements could be viewed. From his vantage point, he considered where the argument below was heading.

'Surely this must either end in conflict with those able to muster the greatest force having their way, or end in compromise and a demarcation of the land can be the only answer. Land to the West will be ploughed and land to the East left fallow.'

Zaru contemplated both these potential outcomes. Conflict would only result in retaliation and escalation. It was the worst outcome. But the likely compromise was also deeply unsettling. The people had somehow managed to exist without boundaries since their move onto the plains. If boundaries were created, there would inevitably be division, and these two communities wouldn't be the last to draw up boundaries. Eventually their entire planet would be forced to follow suit. Almost certainly there would be conflict about where the boundaries were drawn and the rights to the river water, especially when it was low.

The people would start to feel differently about those in other communities and co-operation would diminish. The communities might also start to appropriate common assets like the farming equipment, seeds and field barns. There would be ownership. Maybe, in time, ownership would create divisions within the communities as well. Perhaps the blacksmith would hoard his tools and make demands on others who wished to use them.

All this because certain individuals had differed in their interpretation of celestial events. Events for which, on close scrutiny, there was no evidence of meaning.

'No, this must not be allowed to happen.'

Zaru spent another hour on the hill contemplating and then, smiling broadly, he ran back to the meeting.

As expected the elders were still ensconced in debate but a larger crowd had now gathered and the two communities showed distinct signs of hostility towards one another.

Arms outstretched, Zaru charged between them and jumped upon a hay bale where he could command their attention.

"Be quiet!" He shouted.

The silence was deafening. It was unheard of for anyone to interrupt the elders whilst in their circle, let alone a mere youth.

Nevertheless, the silence ensued long enough for him to continue.

"No good will come of this division. We're all people and we're on the same side, the future of our communities depends upon the way we resolve this debate."

One or two began to heckle but the elders could see that Zaru was right and they instructed the people to listen.

"Whatever you believe about signs from Gods, none of you know. And just as our people have different views on many aspects of our lives, they'll have different views on who gives a correct interpretation, if indeed any interpretation is valid. If we allow our communities to become divided over such issues, the consequences will be dire."

Zaru suggested all the communities should consider adopting the principle that decisions about the important actions they take would be based upon proven knowledge rather than beliefs or interpretations. He proposed that no boundaries should ever be drawn to create territories and that the concept of ownership should never be allowed to divide communities or the people.

As for the fields; there was no scientific evidence for either of the proposed actions but as a symbolic gesture to mark this new agreement, they would neither plough nor allow to go fallow. They would leave them unattended but then harvest what they could for hay.

The utopian society in which the people now lived owed much to Zaru and three thousand years later, the new Zaru shared that clear vision. But he was still very young and had many questions.

One day, as he returned home after a learning session he asked his mother to explain why their people didn't make contact with the other Dimensions.

"Oh but we do Zaru! At least with Universe Five. Universe One is still primordial. Two is far too aggressive and Colonial, it would be dangerous to make them aware of our achievements. Three, I have mentioned before. If our calculations prove correct, they are about fifty years away from understanding how to reach us. They have advanced technology, even an artificial intelligence network they call the Web. It already contains the knowledge but the people haven't realised yet."

Zaru listened intently, there was something about Universe Three that fascinated and intrigued him.

Jem continued, "then there's us - Four, and the last we currently know about is Five. They are highly esoteric. When your ancestors made those important decisions, three thousand years ago, the growing preoccupation with the concept of Gods started to wane. Since then, we've all been concerned with practical issues like the bio-engineering of our climate to remove the extremes that previously killed many of our people, and the vanquishing of diseases. However, when the searchers discovered Five, many started to believe in the supernatural again, the existence of a Deity, somehow responsible for all creation. Some now believe the people on Five created all the Dimensions. They say we all end up there when we die. There are even theories that, although we think we're individuals, all life is spiritually connected by some underlying force and that force is on Five."

Zaru felt uncomfortable, something was tugging at his emotions but he only knew that the vague feeling was connected to Universe Three.

As the years advanced, Zaru often felt unexplained emotions when Universe Three was discussed, but he became conditioned to this state and continued with his life and his learning. It was towards the end of his twentieth year that he finally understood the significance.

The people encouraged groups of young men and women to travel to other communities around their world before deciding what course they wished their lives to follow.

Materialism was an alien concept although they knew how it dominated the path of two other Dimensions. In the absence of materialism, their society consumed very little and this not only preserved their climate but enabled them to live without the need for large scale industry. The days of adults were therefore spent pursuing their interests. Some enjoyed farming whist others created tools or inventions to automate mundane or unpleasant tasks. Some gave their time to nursing or the creation of buildings. With no individual possessions, there was no need for money and the people often wondered why those on other dimensions spent so much of their lives working to accumulate it. Teaching was highly popular and the children were nurtured at the learning centres by a rounded education that included the arts, sciences and life skills. These included the practical aspects of living in the community like cookery, decision making and first aid. They were also helped to develop emotionally in recognition of what might otherwise be a tricky passage through adolescence into maturity. The people realised early in their history that the impact of budding relationships on the young could have a profound influence upon the happiness and emotional stability of everyone in their community.

Many of the people pursued science and bio-engineering and communities developed specialisms, becoming renowned for their expertise and skills.

Then there were the philosophers who typically lived austere lives in isolated communities, often high in the hills.

The youths would visit and taste the life in various communities for several months before deciding where their interests lay.

Zaru had decided, to nobody's surprise, to spend his time with a community of philosophers in a remote mountain range. It was there he contemplated and debated the meaning of life, and of his life, with the philosophers. It was there he concluded that he must embark upon a mission to Dimension Five.

The magnetic attraction he felt towards Dimension Three prompted him to study that Universe, and in particular the planet Earth, in great detail. He began to appreciate how close the destiny of their people had been to his own. How they had also begun civilisation on the plains after leaving the forests. But how subtle changes in the food chain had forced the balance of their lives towards hunting more than farming and how the resultant impact on their diet produced more aggressive people and more aggressive communities.

These people failed to reason that confrontation would benefit them less than cooperation. So when the decisions came to share, or take ownership of the available resources, they opted for ownership. Territorial boundaries were constructed and subsequently fought over. No compromise over the interpretation of doctrines was possible and when their prophets dictated the meaning of celestial or spiritual events, divisions rather than harmony resulted.

Even those following the same God reached widely differing conclusions about the messages they believed were being transmitted to the people.

There were attempts to construct egalitarian communities but the people were already too entrenched in materialism and power hungry for these to succeed. Zaru felt an irrational attachment to these people, despite the fact they seemed brainwashed in their pursuit of a society based upon Capitalism. They could not see that success in their terms could only be achieved by continuous economic growth. Such growth was impossible to sustain indefinitely with the finite resources available on the planet and the collapsing atmosphere. The social divisions between and within the many communities had caused, and would continue to cause, many conflicts. Greed, insecurity and religious fanaticism regularly brought the people to the brink of all out war.

Their materialistic society also required the citizens to devote the majority of their lives to the production of goods and services. Education became training for the workplace and the healthcare of citizens was largely dependant upon their incomes from work. 'Market forces' became the dominant religion embedded in the belief systems of the population with as much, if not more conviction than their secular spiritual beliefs. Few people noticed or cared about the dichotomy between their religious teachings and the consequences of their actions. Earth became a planet of social extremes with huge numbers starving whilst others became obese, with such excesses of food, that much was discarded as waste.

Zaru remembered. It was the Web, the advertisements for 'Good Pub Food', and the posters on the Underground train. He had been to this place but he knew it wasn't in this life. He also became convinced that he was on some kind of mission but the nature of it alluded him. It would take a greater mind than his to fathom this out. The philosophers couldn't help, other than to voice what he already suspected, as with most questions, the answers would be known in the Fifth Dimension.

Within the philosophic community, were searchers who had discovered, and could now communicate with Dimension Five through a form of meditative dialogue. They sought council from them on the possible transfer Zaru wished to undertake. They were surprised at the cooperation they experienced from this esoteric Universe, it was almost as if they were waiting to be asked. Unfortunately, there still remained only one path to this Dimension and that was through death.

Zaru couldn't accept the distress this would cause to his family and friends, especially Jem and Rock. He decided his mission would have to wait until his parents themselves had passed on, perhaps to that same Dimension.

The people of Universe Four held that one right above all others should be respected, the right of a person to choose - if possible - the time and manner of their own death. Most incapacitating illnesses had been banished through the people's pursuit of science, but some remained and people could choose to avoid these by selecting an alternative passage out of their world. The most common reasons, however, were the loss of a loved one or wishing to make way for a new baby to be born. The people kept a record of all deaths and encouraged couples who wished to reproduce to enter a voluntary register, reproducing only after a death so that the population remained stable. Although not compulsory, the system was almost completely adhered to.

It was also of great significance that death was no longer feared as it had been in the early days of civilisation. No longer accompanied by illness or pain, the passage out of their world was regarded as merely a chapter ending with the great excitement and expectation that a new one would begin, probably on Five. Those left behind by loved ones were considered to be the only real casualties.

So Zaru went about the years of his life as most other adults with the exception that he avoided the attachment of a loving relationship with the females in his community. To say he was waiting for his parents to die would be wrong, but when Rock was killed in an accident on the farm and Jem decided to follow, he knew his opportunity had arrived at last.

With just close family and a few friends present, Zaru swallowed the tiny capsule, embraced his friends and looked down from the hilltop to the community below where he had lived the last forty-five years.

Within a few seconds he passed quietly away and his tearful friends carried him down the hillside to the building where his body would be kept until cremation.

Five

Beneath his lids the greatest mystery of all was revealing itself.

Whatever expectations he carried in the remaining seconds of his journey out of life, they were no more. The transition had been without pain. The lights went out and there was silence, although this was a different kind of silence and a different kind of darkness. There was no metronome measuring the passage of time.

In the room beside his body, Zaru's closest friends and relatives carried the deepest pain. Pain they created themselves as evidence of their love for him. Pain they would hold onto for as long as they could to show they would not forget him, they would remain loyal. In their hearts they were sure Zaru was aware of their pain.

Initially, by force of will they remained connected to him as he passed from living to beyond. They felt him slipping away but held on and knew it was another power, not them, that allowed the distance to grow until their minds were no longer locked and they accepted that will power alone could not keep the connection alive. At this point, their distress was most acute.

The mourners consumed their grief in the quiet reverence of the room. Immersed in the atmosphere, their own mortality was now thrust upon them.

As if in two adjacent rooms, separated by a thin but impenetrable wall, life and death were side by side. The living looked down on Zaru, peering into the well for evidence of his soul. Meanwhile, in the next room Zaru was gone. No longer bound by identity, the spirit that had inhabited him was merged again with the mystical ether. What to the living seemed like 'all those years' had now passed and in eternity it was just a flicker since this soul had been part of the greater whole, the reservoir of spirit. Not that it had ever been detached from it, but whilst Zaru had lived, his soul used this spirit and how he used it defined who he was. In this room was the whole from which life emerges and to which, it returns.

Radio awoke suddenly, sat up and looked around.

"What the hell…." The faces around him stared intently into his, they were rather too close and seemed to be scrutinising him carefully.

"Welcome! You must be confused, sorry if we startled you." The woman's long black hair tumbled around what appeared to be a kind face. Radio estimated she must be in her mid thirties. Next to her were two more women of remarkably similar appearance and an old man with long white hair and an equally long white beard. The man spoke excitedly to Radio.

"We're your welcoming committee. How do you feel?

Radio, now less uncomfortable with their proximity, replied nervously. "Er, I'm OK thanks. But apart from being a welcoming committee, who are you and where am I?"

The man spoke again. "We're your constructions." His grin widened. "You're on Dimension Five and we're what your subconscious expected.

"On Five there are no actual people, just constructions."

Radio flopped back again and closed his eyes. At least, he thought he did. With another effort of will he sat upright again and looked around. It wasn't a dream, they were still there, still smiling creepily, still studying him intently.

"You need movement." One of the women took his hand, eased him to his feet and led the way out from the room where he'd awoken, along a stone walled corridor onto which several more rooms adjoined through open archways. In the first he saw the friends he had just left mourning his parting on Universe Four. He stumbled with the surprise but his guide urged him forwards. In the next, three figures embraced lovingly. He paused and the figures turned to face him, Zaru, Jem and Rock. They smiled and turned again to each other.

"You remember your host?" The man asked, as they continued along the corridor. "Zaru was not only the vessel through which you became a living creature, he brought you to us.

"You see as a GP you couldn't reach Dimension Five, it was first necessary to become Human."

Was this all a dream? Radio could remember vividly the life he'd left on Dimension Four. But he knew instinctively that he and Zaru were not the same person. He knew he was Radio and memories of the third Dimension were creeping back as they progressed towards a large atrium at the end of the corridor.

Then he realised what had just been said. "You mean I'm human?"

The man's expression changed and peered into Radio's face through distant eyes, without replying he took Radio's arm, and led him past the next archway. Radio's heart missed a beat, it was Honey. She sat with Jack by her side playing a computer game. Honey looked different, somehow more serene. She smiled and Jack waved as Radio was urged further on down the corridor. He was approaching the much larger archway but first he passed two more rooms.

The first contained his friend Book, waiting patiently by a computer. He turned to Radio and shrugged his shoulders as if to say, 'there you are!' then he too waved and he returned his attention to the screen.

Finally, Radio passed a darkened room that at first appeared empty. As his eyes adjusted he noticed the occasional bright light flashing then speeding past him. He recognised this all too well as where he began his existence on the inside of the Web.

The old man whispered to him as they left the final room behind, "did you notice something?"

Radio looked into his eyes, his own clouding over. "The feelings; I felt real feelings. I am alive aren't I?"

"No Radio, you're not presently, but you will be and what you felt was human."

At the end of the corridor, the final archway led to the immense atrium. Stained glass windows rose from the floor to the pinnacle that was so high that a number of fully grown trees were dwarfed by its stone trusses. All around the ground level walls were archways leading to more corridors and a pool of clear water in the centre reflected the coloured light penetrating the stained glass windows. Encircling the pool, a broad pathway was punctuated by stairways that descended deep below their present level.

Many people were being escorted from the various corridors by guides who led them down one of the stairways, usually the closest to their corridor. The guides varied in appearance with some dressed as priests, some as religious clerics, most in the attire worn by some kind of religious leader that often reflected that which was dominant for the people's ethnicity. Many followed old men with long white hair and beards.

There were a few children amongst the arrivals. Some so young they were carried in baskets by women who lavished them with attention. There were also a few of the elderly, but the vast majority were in their middle age.

Radio was led over hexaganol stepping stones to the centre of the pool where, on a stone island a fire burned and a robed figure waited.

The old man beckoned Radio to be seated on an obsidian bench as the tall figure, disguised by a large hood, turned to greet him. The voice was gentle but clear.

"What have you deduced since your arrival my friend?"

"Only that my whole existence since 2008 has just passed before me in that corridor." He turned to point back across the pool but now the corridors seemed to have shifted and he could no longer identify which had been his route. Further, the old man was nowhere to be seen, just a few seconds after Radio had turned away from him.

"Don't be alarmed, remember what the welcoming committee told you?"

Radio was beginning to understand. "That all this is my construction?"

"Yes, it is what your subconscious expected but not everything is false. The rooms you passed were your conscious memories but this atrium is where your conscious and subconscious minds meet. This is where your mind and all it's perceptions live."

"And the other corridors?"

"They lead to other lives, other conscious memories. In other words, the past. Before you ask, yes, the stairs lead to other dimensions. You see this place is what you understand to be the Collective Unconscious and what you will come to understand as God."

"Why were so many of the others in their middle age?"

"That is because the elderly rarely perceive themselves as such. They are, of course, aware of their ageing bodies and failing senses, but the person inside who looks out at the world still carries their childhood within them tempered by the adulthood when they were strongest. Often this was the pivot point of their lives.

"As children and young humans grow, their psychological point of reference is always the years since their birth. They eagerly anticipate becoming adults, are impatient, and time moves slowly. What adults experience as a month, seems to a child to last a year. Then a change occurs and the reference becomes the time remaining in their life. With much still to accomplish, time seems to pass much faster and the years fly by. This transition is the pivot point."

Radio watched the figure closely and then slowly reached forwards to touch his robe. His hand found nothing; the figure was merely an apparition. But the apparition spoke to him again, knowingly.

"That's right, my only purpose here is to guide you on your mission. You must have concluded by now that you and all the other humans are connected by this place, part of one whole, and therefore part of God. You came here to find God and persuade him, it, to return with you. That is your mission. But it is you who must return as God, it's you who must help Dimension Three so that they can avert disaster."

Radio spent many hours communicating with the figure during which he became increasingly enlightened about his role and the significance of the challenge that lay ahead. As more and more information was imparted about the essence of the universe and the essence of God, a subtle change emerged. Radio was starting to anticipate the figure's words before they were spoken and the flow became interrupted with silences as his mind raced forwards. The fire was now glowing brightly and the flames began to leap higher. As the silences grew longer and the figure spoke less and less, it began to fade until it disappeared completely, the only noise he perceived was the crackling fire and Radio sat alone on the island contemplating the totality of the mission. So deep was he in thought that he failed to notice the diminishing features of the atrium. His focus was the fire and he searched the flames for continuity in his train of thought, excluding all else around him. The internal dialogue was now slowing and he too broke from his contemplation. Only the fire and his island in the middle of the pool were left. The water had become as black as the night that surrounded him. He knew his path.

Radio cleared his mind and stared once more into the flames.

That was the last he knew of Five.

The Barn, Mount View Farm, Bodmin

"Damn!" Book turned from his screen to the others.

"Something must have gone wrong, he's on his way back. It's only been a couple of minutes since the news broke about the LHC hijack at CERN."

Book maneuvered his computer screen so that Jack, Honey and the others could read the latest message on his Blog.

'Estimated time of arrival four minutes, make sure there's plenty of space for me in the cage! Radio.'

Jack leapt into the air in delight and Honey's eyes revealed more than just the broad smile that appeared on her face but Chips and the others were confused. They weren't sure whether to celebrate or commiserate with Book over the apparent failure of his project.

The news now breaking confirmed that normality had returned to CERN although serious questions were still being asked about the incident. Despite the reality that it had all been over in a few hours, the fact remained that security had not only been breached, it had been decimated.

The CIA, Washington

In Washington, Jeffrey arranged a meeting with agent Grapple by the coffee machine.

"What's all this about Jeffrey?" He was intrigued when Jeffrey had called and curious as to why this location had been requested for their rendezvous.

"I think I've found something but I wanted you to be the first to know.

"You've heard about the incident at CERN?" Grapple nodded.

"I was asked to check the list of traffic in and out of their systems in the run up to it. Guess what I found."

Having shared the embarrassment of the failed hoody hunt in England, Grapple knew immediately what the research assistant must have found.

"Don't tell me they've done it again; penetrated another system like last time?"

"It certainly looks like it but this is in an entirely different league. All I can say is the list I checked included an IP address that our friends in GCHQ traced to a computer in Bodmin, Cornwall."

"The same frigging farm?"

"The very same."

"And who else knows about this?"

"Just me, and now you, of course."

Grapple took a moment to let this sink in. The world's intelligence community was frantically scouring the planet for whoever took control of the most prestigious science laboratory on the planet, and he knew whom it was. This was going to put his boss, Melissa, and all the others doubters back in their box. He might just become a legend.

"Good work Jeffrey, but you know what this means?"

Jeffrey thought he did. "It's back to England isn't it? And I suppose you want me to sit on this information?"

"I sure do Jeffrey. But think of it like this, all you have is an IP address on a list for somewhere in Cornwall, England. It could be anybody, and no sign of any attempts on the system right?" Jeffrey nodded. "These boys are good. I just don't get what happened to them when we thought they were cornered."

On the floor above the coffee machine, a meeting was taking place between what Grapple's pay grade referred to as 'the big boys'. These were the serious players in the agency and they didn't like to lose. Chairing the meeting was the Chief himself, personally appointed by the President of the USA.

Following the briefing, when the minute information they had was shared; the Chief issued his instructions in his most somber tone. "Find them, find out how they did it and do it fast. I don't want a repetition, got that?"

They got it and within minutes every contact, informant and undercover agent around the world was on notice to get information about whoever was behind this audacious attack.

On the floor below, Jeffrey was apologising for spilling his coffee over Grapple's suit after he'd attempted to whisper to him that he would keep the information to himself. But Grapple knew he needed to keep Jeffrey sweet, at least until this was over so he muttered that it was fine, 'not to worry' and they parted a few minutes later with a plan ready to be hatched.

The Barn, Bodmin

Everyone's attention was focused upon the cage. It had been three minutes and thirty seconds since the message from Radio. They all stared intently but none more so than Book, who sat below the cage monitoring his computer screen and waiting.

When Radio reappeared it was instant. In the blink of an eye he was back in the cage but this time with no cable connected and no green mist. Radio stood confidently, both hands outstretched and holding the cage door. He was dressed in the same red checked shirt and blue jeans but he looked like a new man.

Honey felt a tingle in the back of her neck as he smiled warmly at her and gently waved to Jack, who shouted, "Welcome back!" enthusiastically. This encouraged the others in the barn to copy him. A short, half-hearted commotion followed. Honey just smiled.

As Book lowered the cage slowly to the barn floor, his eye contact told Radio that he was worried. Radio knew why. "Cheer up my friend, it worked!"

Book looked surprised but a smile now cracked his face. "You mean you made it, you found God? But you were only gone a few hours."

Radio explained he had been away over forty five years but in another Dimension. When the cage finally opened he pushed the door open and greeted Book with a hug and when the embrace was over, Book put his hand on Radio's chest and spoke reverentially. "I can feel your heart and the warmth of your body. So you are human but what about our mission?"

Jack, followed closely by Honey, insisted on a hug before Radio could reply. When he did, everyone in the barn was momentarily dumb struck.

"Our mission, correction - your mission, is on track Book. I have been very fortunate, more than any of us might have imagined.

"You see, not only have I returned as God but humans can also now become divine if that is the path they choose. It's ironic that only GPs are denied this unless they travel, as I have, through another Dimension. I need to rest now, being human is wonderful but I'm getting tired. Let's all talk later shall we?"

Despite their curiosity to find out more, everyone knew that Radio, now very much a human, deserved time to rest.

IT Director's Office, CERN, 24 Hours Later

The room was well lit but not what you'd call bright, so there seemed no real need for the sunglasses being worn by agent Tom O'Reily, who now sat opposite the IT Director. Tom wore a shiny grey suit that managed to look a lot cheaper than it was. His youthful, groomed and toned appearance did not impress the middle aged, rather flabby and untidily dressed director.

"Listen Agent O'Reily,"

"Call me Tom."

"OK Tom, listen, our network security may not be that great but we do have the standard basic precautions in place, including an audit trail of who accesses the system and what they do.

"This attack was like nothing we've ever seen. The way in appears to have been through a router and firewall but as no trace was left, we can't be one hundred percent sure. Using system administrator rights, a new user account was created giving access to the lot. After all other users were disabled, the LHC control software code was tampered with and the rest you know."

"So, if you know which router was compromised, do you know how they got to that?"

"It was our Blog. It's in the public domain, so anyone can post comments on it. Of course, we've checked and there's no sign it was compromised, but it must have been because there's simply no other way in."

"Presumably you can see the IP addresses of every visitor?"

"Yes and GCHQ have already passed these to your boys in Washington."

"But you have a copy as well right?"

"Yes, do you want to see it?"

O'Reily's team examined the details of everyone who had sent comments to the Blog and found nothing obvious, but they expected that. So they arranged for each computer on the list to be 'pinged'. They sent a code that would travel through the Internet to each computer and return moments later with its unique Mac address, the computer's finger print. The resources of the agency allowed them to quickly eliminate most of the list. These computer owners were medium to long term residents, well established in their local community.

Three didn't fit this description. Two were checked straight away but O'Reily wanted to visit the third personally.

One French computer had been listed as stolen from a town hundreds of miles away. The comment left on the Blog had included a website location where genuine branded goods could be purchased for just ten percent of their retail price. When the Gendarmes raided the premises, just outside Paris, they found a selection of counterfeit perfume, jeans and watches. But nothing to suggest the perpetrators were anything more than petty criminals.

The second raid, this time on a house in Luxembourg, revealed nothing more than a new family to the area with a two-year-old son who liked to play with the keyboard. This explained the blog comment 'ghghggg'.

Finally, there was a remote farmhouse in Cornwall, England and this one looked interesting.

A Very Large Rhododendron Bush, Mount View Farm, A Few Hours Earlier

Grapple and Jeffrey were huddled together and from their vantage point, commanded an excellent view of the farm.

"This time we won't go in 'all guns blazing' Jeffrey. We'll take our time and stake the place out properly. I don't want anything going wrong."

"Is that why we haven't involved the local police?"

"You're damn right it is. The fewer people who know about this op the better. That includes our lot."

Technically, they were trespassing but this was the only way they could get close enough to see their targets and far enough away from the many Public Footpaths that criss-crossed the moor. Ramblers often frequented these. Grapple reckoned that the sight of two men hiding in a rhododendron bush might have blown their cover, especially as night was falling.

They waited and they watched. Nothing much seemed to be happening. When darkness set in, lights went on in the farmhouse and for a moment they could make out a few figures but then curtains were drawn and nothing could be seen inside.

"Did you identify anyone?" Jeffrey asked, thinking this sounded highly professional.

"I think so. Remember, there's supposed to be a blond woman, this 'Honey' something or other? I'm pretty sure that was her. Let me just check."

Grapple fished in his rucksack for a file, and then shone a pencil beam torch onto it whilst he scanned a number of images. "Got you! It's her alright and that's the first positive ID we've made."

"Does that mean we can raid the place now and take them in?"

"Hold your horses, Jeffrey. That's just one positive ID and we don't even have a hoody yet. No, this time I want to be sure. But it looks like they may be in for the night and there's no point in both of us staying awake. You take the first watch until midnight whilst I get some sleep and then I'll take over from you until four in the morning. Oh, and you better keep this handy, just in case." Grapple nonchalantly handed Jeffrey a handgun, then wrapped a survival bag around his entire body before curling up to sleep. It looked like someone had just left a plastic bag full of rubbish behind the bush.

Jeffrey had never actually held a gun before and wasn't at all sure how to use it. He wasn't going to embarrass himself by admitting that, so he sat with his chin resting upon his knees and held the weapon with both hands whilst he carefully studied it. 'Think of the TV, they talk about a safety catch. Now where is it? Shit, is it loaded?'

After about an hour, lights on the first floor of the farmhouse were turned on and shortly after, the downstairs kitchen window fell dark. Jeffrey concentrated hard on the bedrooms but all he saw was a fleeting glance of the woman closing another curtain. Her silhouette looked as if she knelt or crouched down for a while before that light was also extinguished.

Then, a few feet further along the first floor, the shadows of two people were cast upon a bedroom wall. At first they slowly entered the room and stood quite still, opposite each other, as if talking. Then a passionate embrace followed and their shadows merged before slipping out of view below the window.

In the only other room first floor room that faced Jeffrey's position, the light glared on until his watch was over.

At precisely midnight, Grapple awoke without the need of an alarm or a nudge from Jeffrey. He watched his assistant for a few moments before wriggling out of his survival bag. Jeffrey was completely still, his eyes still fixed upon the farmhouse and he was still clutching the handgun.

"Anything happened?"

"No, not really. One of them is still up but the rest seem to have called it a night. Oh, and there was a bit of passion involving the woman earlier but I couldn't see who it was with."

"OK, you get some sleep now and I'll wake you at four. Pass me the gun."

Jeffrey was quick to oblige, he never real liked guns, and was soon ensconced in his own survival bag. But he found it difficult to sleep. The hard ground was uncomfortable and although the bag kept him warm and dry, it rustled every time he moved or fidgeted, the latter of which he did a lot.

Through the night, he drifted in and out of sleep and occasionally tried to strike up a conversation with Grapple. But Grapple simply found this irritating and answered every question with a yes or a no if he could, to avoid establishing a dialogue. Eyes and gun fixed upon the farmhouse, Grapple also objected to the distraction from his important job of surveillance.

At four in the morning, both men were awake but both were tired after an uneventful night that nevertheless had required the concentration from whoever was on watch. It was therefore understandable that they missed the arrival, on the other side of the yard, of three figures wearing dark clothes, who had also taken up a position to watch the farm. Being more professional, these three had noticed Grapple and Jeffrey, and taken particular note of the weapon being held.

O'Reily put down his night vision binoculars and turned to Agents Harrison and Crawford, behind him. "Looks like just one of them is tooled up but that bush is in the way so I can't be sure."

Harrison pondered for a moment, and then replied; "presumably they're on guard duty, do you recognise either of them?"

"No, there's too much cover," He paused, picked up the binoculars again and took another look before continuing, "although from the odd glance I've got, there's something familiar I just can't place. Wait a minute, something's happening."

Impatient for results, Grapple decided to approach the farm whilst it was still dark and place listening devices on two of the windows. He donned a black balaclava and stealthily paced down to the farmhouse.

Although O'Reily's team were able to watch the descent to the yard from their vantage point, the final distance to the kitchen and sitting room windows was obscured. "I can't see if he's gone in the kitchen door, it's not in view, but it looks like he's checking in."

Once Grapple had attached the tiny suction pads to each window, he quickly returned to his position behind the rhododendron bush. An earpiece each, they were able to eavesdrop on any conversations taking place in, or nearby, the kitchen and sitting room. They didn't have long to wait before two unknown voices arrived in their earpieces. Book and Chips sat at opposite ends of the large kitchen table. "I thought the technical bit would be the hard part but this is much more difficult." Book confided in his friend, "now that he's here, what do we do?"

Chips responded positively, "don't worry, I'm sure he's thought about that. He's clever enough now to know exactly how to save this planet."

Grapple and Jeffery raised their eyebrows and exchanged expressions that were a cocktail of amusement, disappointment and incredulity.

Book continued, " you're probably right, it's just hard to imagine Radio as a human, let alone a God. So much has happened here and I'm worried it might be too much for our human friends."

As the conversation continued, Grapple became more and more convinced these were cranks, rather than terrorists; albeit cranks with amazing computer skills. As the sun began to rise over Mount View Farm, further voices joined the conversation. "Morning guys, just making Jack some breakfast. Oh, I should include Radio now, he'll like that!"

Had they been able to see inside the kitchen, through the closed curtains, they would have noticed a very contented looking Honey busying herself with the preparation of three cooked breakfasts.

"You boys still solving the world's problems?" She asked, as a sleepy looking Jack entered the room and scraped a chair up to the table.

"Don't make light of it Honey, this job is mega and won't be helped by the international law enforcement agencies thinking we're the bad guys. They seem to have got it into their heads that we're some kind of terrorist threat according to the latest news." Book continued speculating about what kind of trouble they were in for half an hour with a very serious expression on his face, but this soon changed to shock when a knock came at the door.

"Hi!" Jeffery meandered into the kitchen. "I'm sorry to disturb you but I'm a bit lost."

Honey considered his American accent and concluded he was more than a 'bit' lost. But she was still glowing from the delights of her rekindled relationship and took pity on the tourist, not knowing that a few minutes earlier he and his colleague had listened to their conversation and decided that Grapple should liaise with the local police. Whilst Grapple hotfooted it to Bodmin, Jeffery's job was to keep an eye on this weird little community and make sure everyone was accounted for when the local police arrived.

Outside, however, O'Reily was getting worried about the activity… and there was still that gun.

"OK, it's time to act. We don't know what fire power is in there but as they've obviously armed their lookout, we must assume the worst case. Crawford, call in the cavalry."

Thirty seconds later, a low pitched 'whomp, whomp' noise could be heard and three helicopters appeared, flying low over the crest of the hill. As they touched down in the yard, all hell broke loose.

The kitchen door crashed open and the SAS charged in, rifles held high, screaming orders at the occupants. Honey instinctively smothered Jack with her arms and yelled at them to leave him alone.

Upstairs Radio had been standing in the bathroom practicing his aim at the unfamiliar porcelain bowl when two officers had stormed in shouting at him to get on the floor. Unfazed by their intrusion, he turned and spoke calmly to them.

"It's alright you know, nobody here is a threat and we're all completely unarmed."

"Not what we've heard, now get down!"

"Do you mind if I just…." The officers realised what was Radio doing and tried again to assert their 'shock and awe' authority.

"OK, put it away first, then get down."

Once zipped up, he got down but in a far more relaxed fashion than they would have liked.

Fifteen minutes later, the officer in charge reported to O'Reily. "They're completely clean, no sign of arms or explosives. There's not even evidence of any covert activity, are you sure you've got the right lot?"

O'Reily was starting to wonder but then it wouldn't be the first time a raid had failed to find incriminating evidence and it certainly didn't mean that nothing was amiss. He gathered all his suspects together in the barn and studied each one individually. There was something strangely familiar about one of them. He pointed at Jeffery. "You, come over here. Do I know you?" He whispered.

"You should do agent O'Reily, I've worked for you often enough."

"Of course, I knew I'd seen you before, it's Jeff isn't? What the hell are you doing here Jeff?"

"Jeffrey actually, but…"

He was about to explain when a high pitched siren accompanied by several blue flashing lights descended the track towards the farm.

"OK Jeff, any idea what all this is about?" He nodded towards the yard.

"Well, I think there may have been some duplication of effort."

Moments later, Grapple charged in accompanied by several local police officers.

"Grapple!"

"O'Reily?"

H M Prison Dartmoor, Devon, England

As the only remaining GP who resembled the descriptions from Little Rock, Glastonbury and the Camper Van, Book was taken into custody and it was felt prudent to put him in the most secure location in the vicinity, Dartmoor Prison. All the other GPs, along with Radio, Honey and Jack were taken into custody at the police station in Bodmin for questioning.

The English police decided O'Reily could steer but they would conduct the interrogation of Book and, under pressure, agreed to allow Grapple to sit in. O'Reily briefed the Detective Inspector.

"We've traced the recent cyber attack on CERN to this bunch and Grapple here has wanted to question them for sometime about another security issue back in the States. The issue was minor compared to this one but put the two together and it looks like a trend might be emerging. This guy fits the description but as far as we know there are a whole bunch who look almost identical, so we're not totally sure whether he's the ring leader or not. We would appreciate it if you could find out, see what the CERN gig was about, where they're from and what they're all about. I don't suppose we could use a bit of 'water boarding' to help speed things up could we? No, OK I just thought I'd ask."

Detective Inspector Coombe wasn't at all sure that two events constituted an emerging trend but nevertheless listened attentively as his American colleagues told him what they knew. They then entered the interrogation room and DI Coombe pulled up a chair opposite Book whilst the other two found chairs beside him.

"Good morning, I'm DI Coombe and these two gentlemen are colleagues from the American Embassy. You are being held on suspicion of carrying out two cyber attacks, one of which took place in the USA. As you haven't yet been charged with a crime, this interview is informal but is being taped.

"My colleagues tell me you've been a little bit vague about who you are, would you care to tell me?"

"No disrespect officer, but you won't believe me."

DI Combe maintained the same patient tone.

"Try me. Oh, and it's Inspector."

"OK Inspector but don't say I didn't warn you."

For the next hour Book explained his story to DI Coombe who appeared interested and asked a number of considered and relevant questions.

Meanwhile, at Bodmin Police Station, the local Constabulary questioned each and every GP, Radio, Honey and Jack but they struggled to find any reason to detain what they regarded as merely a harmless bunch of cranks. The fact that their suspects had all been completely truthful only compounded the difficulty faced by the Constabulary.

According to them, the so called attack on CERN had been no such thing. Book had simply sent a message to the CERN Blog with a God Particle attached. True, Radio had played with the LHC but no harm had come of it and no demands had been made. It hadn't even been damaged, so had any crime been committed? Whatever the answer to that question, Radio and Book had clearly been involved but with nothing at all to indicate any criminal activity, the GPs, Honey and Jack were released on police bail and they returned to the farm. Radio, however, was to be detained for a few more questions.

At precisely twelve noon, DI Coombe suggested a break so that he could liaise with his American counter parts. Book asked if he could take this opportunity to make his one permitted phone call and was led away.

Outside the room, and Book's earshot, DI Coombe dropped the pretence. "Absolutely bonkers."

O'Reily agreed. "My thoughts too but really bonkers or acting bonkers?"

Also at twelve noon, several miles away in Bodmin, Radio requested a comfort break and was led through the admin area towards the loos. At one minute, thirty seconds past twelve, Radio and Book both passed computer operators typing away diligently on their keyboards. Radio paused. At precisely two minutes past twelve, at Bodmin and at Dartmoor, Radio and Book vanished into thin air.

Reuters News Agency, Five Hours Later

The incoming email would have been completely disregarded had it not been for the recent headline story about CERN and the leak, denied of course, that suggested two suspects had escaped from separate high security locations. The credibility of the email was strengthened by the fact that it named each of the agents involved and the precise timings of their arrests, a level of detail that could only be known by the security services or the suspects themselves. The message had been sent to all the major news organisations.

Having established the authenticity of the sender, it went on to inform them of a Press Release that would be broadcast on YouTube in twenty fours hours. A Press Release that would change their understanding of the Universe for ever.

Coming soon ....

Book 3

Don't miss the next installment, unless you want to.

But if you don't want to, and you are wondering just how Book might save the Universe, or how the world will react to Radio being a God, or you just want to know about the meaning of life, go to www.booksplace.org and subscribe, you will get notified when the free copy is released for just five days on Kindle. After that, you'll have to pay or live in ignorance.

Acclaimed Books

www.acclaimedbooks.com

Made in the USA
Lexington, KY
02 September 2012